EPIC KIDS

DAVID BLAZE

For Zander...

Wow! That's Epic!

Contents

ONE

MY LUNCH TRAY
HAS WINGS

I wasn't sure what to do when the cool new kids at school asked me to sit at their lunch table. I had just set my tray down at my usual spot, you know, the not-so-cool table where one kid is always picking his nose and another is wiping greasy pizza hands all over his shirt.

"Do you think you're cool, Jake?" Omar Kim asked from my table. He had long black hair tied back in a ponytail and wore a bright tie-dye T-shirt. "You're not cool." He scooped a spoonful of mashed potatoes, splashed it in gravy, and then swished it through the air like a boomerang. "Get on the gravy plane! Yeah!"

I sighed and glanced at the cool table behind me, where two kids stared at me and waved, waiting for me to join them. It didn't seem real because no one ever picked me for anything.

I wasn't good at sports and was always the last kid

chosen for teams in P.E. Well, I wasn't chosen—I was the last kid left. Just yesterday, I tried to throw a baseball to second base, but it went sideways and nearly took Coach Michael's head off.

I wasn't that great at school either. I had repeated the second grade because my teacher didn't think I had the skills to make it through later grade levels. Even now, I never went home with a perfect report card … I was more of an A, B, and sometimes C student. Okay, mostly C's. And I only got A's in one class—English.

Then there's the school bus situation. Every day was a challenge to find a seat because other kids claimed the seat next to them was reserved. The only thing it was reserved for was their lunches and selfish backpacks.

"See you later," I said to Omar as I picked my tray back up from the table and turned around. He had a habit of making me feel like I would never amount to anything. I hadn't been picked before today, but now it was time to find out what it felt like.

Five seconds later, I was sitting at the cool table, across from the new girl named Amanda. She had long blonde hair and shiny green eyes. She had to be a year or two older than me (I was twelve) because she looked more mature than all the other girls in sixth grade. I didn't know much about her other than she started at this school last week with two boys who were always by her side. One of them was stuck in the lunch line, glaring at me like I'd better run for my life before he got his monstrous hands around my neck.

"Don't worry about him," Amanda said with a straight face. Easy for her to say, but I sat far enough back from the table to make for a quick escape if necessary. The guy in the lunch line was named Darryl. He had arrived here on the same day as Amanda, but I don't care what anyone says, he wasn't a sixth grader like the rest of us, he couldn't be. I wondered if he had repeated the second grade, third, fourth, and fifth. He was over six feet tall and looked like he needed to shave his hairy face.

"Jake doesn't belong here," the only other kid at the table said, shaking his head at Amanda and waving me off. I wasn't sure what he had against me, and I couldn't figure out how he fit in with the other cool kids. He was the last one who had arrived here with Amanda. His name was Tony; he was the yin to Darryl's yang at a noticeably short four feet tall and had the biggest forehead I had ever seen. "He's not like us."

Amanda held up a hand for him to be silent.

He huffed like a frustrated kindergartener and stood up to point at my usual table. I turned to see Omar and the other guys flinging mashed potatoes and gravy at each other, laughing and snorting like happy pigs playing in filthy mud. "That's where he came from. Those kids are morons."

"Back off," I warned him. "Those are my friends." I was surprised when he sat back down without an argument. He squinted at me and kept eating his lunch.

"I've been watching you," Amanda said to me. "You always stand up for others. Why?"

I shrugged and said, "I'm not better than anyone else."

She caught Tony's attention and nodded.

"So," he said to me reluctantly, wiping the sides of his mouth with a napkin, "we're all going to see the latest *Party Marty* movie tomorrow morning in Spring Rock." Spring Rock was the town next to ours and more than thirty miles away. He shook his head slowly like he felt sick by what he was about to say next. "You should come with us."

I was dying to see that movie, but there was a major problem with their plan that made it impractical. "We have school tomorrow."

Tony snickered and put his palms up in the air like he didn't understand what the problem was. He looked around the cafeteria then leaned across the table and motioned for me to come close. "We're not coming to school tomorrow."

Amanda nodded to confirm what he said was true. I felt conflicted because I'd never skipped school and had perfect attendance. Teachers loved me. What would they think of me if I missed a day?

Tony pointed back at my usual lunch table. "Unless you want to stay here and hang out with your weird friends."

Omar was piloting his spoon full of mashed potatoes and gravy through the air again. "Get on the gravy plane!"

I took a deep breath. Could I even consider skipping school? There was a rumor that a teacher guarded the movie theaters to catch any kid trying to escape from class. And if a kid was caught, they were kicked out of school forever. We all knew it wasn't true, but no one was brave enough to test that theory. Besides, I was the kid who always did what he was told to do. I was the kid who stayed out of trouble. But ... I was also the kid who felt like I didn't belong where everyone thought I was supposed to be.

"This is never going to work," Tony warned, tossing his fork onto his tray and crossing his arms. "He's not ready." Amanda stared at him with cold eyes to silence him. It seemed odd to me that he always obeyed.

"What do you want to do?" Amanda asked me, smiling wide while her eyes sparkled again. "I really want you to come with us. You have to be there."

I looked into her eyes, wondering how today went from being a boring school day to a day when I considered doing something I would never have considered before. "I think that—"

A large shadow loomed over the table. I turned to the side and looked up to see Darryl's hairy face.

"Get out of my seat," he demanded. He set his tray down on the table and stood there, staring down at me, waiting for me to stand up and leave. I felt sick because I didn't want to cause any trouble, but I also didn't want to be condemned back to the uncool table.

"He sits here now," Amanda informed him in a stern voice.

"You can't do this! I won't allow it!" Darryl raised a fist to his chest then threw it forward like he was tossing a Frisbee.

That's when things got crazy.

My lunch tray flew off the table and up into the air, higher than my head, then spun around and floated before it dropped and crashed back onto the table in front of me. Milk splashed all over my face and shirt.

I jumped out of my chair and backed away from the table while my chair crashed to the floor behind me with a loud thud. Every movement in the lunchroom seemed to happen in slow motion as kids turned to look at me. My heart and breathing stopped. What I had just seen was impossible!

The lunchroom fell silent; then all the kids pointed at me and laughed, not knowing what had happened before I was dripping wet in milk. At any other time in my life, I would have been embarrassed, but all I could think about was the floating tray. If Darryl and the other new kids were capable of that, then what else were they capable of?

"What's going on here?" the vice principal, Mr. Spradley, asked, standing behind Amanda and shaking his bald head at me. He had a bushy gray mustache to match the gray suit and tie he wore every day. His steel eyes felt eerily familiar to me. Something you should know about Mr. Spradley is some days he loved kids and other days he hated kids. You could never tell what kind of day it was by looking at him because he always smiled.

Amanda stared across the table at Darryl with eyes that told him to be silent. Tony put his hands behind his head, leaned back in his chair, and chuckled. Darryl grabbed the chair from behind me, placed it back at the table, and sat on it, reclaiming his spot. And me? I stood there, lost and confused, milk dripping off my nose, not sure if I could form any words after what had happened.

"You," Mr. Spradley said, pointing at me. "Get your food and go stand up front." That's where he sent all the troublemakers during lunch. They had to face the kids in the cafeteria while standing up, holding their trays, and eating whatever they could without dropping it. I had never expected to go up there.

I tried to explain what had happened, but my mouth was dry, and words felt like rocks scraping against my throat.

"Save your breath," he advised. "I don't want to hear a word out of you. Get up front."

"But—"

"Now!"

I glanced at Darryl, Tony, and Amanda, hoping one of them would say something to save me. Amanda mouthed that she was sorry, and I believed her. I believed she was the only good person at the table I wished I had never sat at.

Maybe Omar Kim was right—I wasn't cool.

I brushed past Mr. Spradley and headed to the front of the cafeteria with the other dozen kids he had sent up there. I lost my breath when I turned around to face the tables filled with kids. Hundreds of them watched me on display as a convicted troublemaker.

I didn't touch my food and waited impatiently

for lunch hour to be over, shifting my weight from one leg to the other so they wouldn't both go numb at the same time. Ten minutes were still left on the clock. Every second was longer than the last one.

Darryl kept turning his head back and forth as he glanced at me then argued with Amanda. I had no idea what his problem was with me or why Amanda seemed to like me. All I knew was he had made my lunch tray fly like a magic carpet, and he didn't look like a magician.

As I watched them, I realized there was something different about the new kids, something magical, something epic. Maybe it made them dangerous, but I had to know more about them. Even after what had just happened, I was drawn to them like cheese to pizza. I had to be part of their group.

There's no way I could skip school though. The teachers would faint, and my mom would send me to school in some foreign country. Everyone expected me to be good and do well all the time, but I hated it. Once, just once, I wanted to do something no one ever expected me to do.

"I didn't do anything wrong," I said to Mr.

Spradley as he marched across the lunch line of delinquents.

He smiled wide and reached for the microphone on the podium he used so the whole lunchroom could hear him. "Hey, everyone!" he shouted in a cheery voice. "Because of Jake, you are all now on silent lunch. Enjoy." He set the microphone back down and said to me, "I told you to save your breath."

All the talking and laughing and horse playing left the lunchroom like a vacuum cleaner had sucked it out. Hundreds of angry eyes stared at me as if they wanted to rip me apart. I gulped and tried not to look at anyone.

Omar jumped out of his chair and ran through the crowd of kids like he was being chased by angry hornets. His tie-dye T-shirt made it hard to miss him. Bits of mashed potatoes and gravy flew off his body with every hurried step. When he reached the front of the cafeteria, Mr. Spradley held his hands out and stopped him.

"There's no running in here!" he shouted like Omar wasn't right in front of him. "Where do you think you're going?"

Omar's face turned blue. He bent over and chunked at least a gallon of vomit all over Mr. Spradley's pants and shoes.

Mr. Spradley stepped back and put his hands up high in the air. "Go on," he said in disgust. "Get out of here."

I couldn't help but laugh. That turned out to be a huge mistake. My laugh was the only noise in the lunchroom because everyone else was still silent. But, come on, Mr. Spradley deserved it!

He used two fingers to motion for the janitor to come over. That guy had messy blond hair that draped over his ears and into his eyes like a surfer. He looked like he was still in high school. "Hey, Janitor Whatever-Your-Name-Is, get a mop and bucket for Jake." Mr. Spradley crossed his arms and glared at me. He shook his legs to get off as much of the slimy mess as he could then headed for the bathroom. "This floor better be shining like pure gold by the time I get back."

The noise in the lunchroom grew loud again as soon as he was out of sight. The janitor took my tray, shoved a mop into my hands, and rolled a mop bucket up to my feet. "Do what I do," he suggested, nodding down at the vomit. "Imagine it's spaghetti." He stepped away but turned right back around and held up a hand. "Don't eat it though. I made that mistake once."

My stomach churned. I dipped the mop in the bucket then chased the vomit as fast as I could. It spread over the floor like a raging river, right to Amanda's table.

She shrieked when it nearly touched her shoes. I jammed the mop under the table and stopped the vomit stream. She was standing in her chair when she thanked me.

"Looking for one of your relatives down there?" Tony asked me, smirking.

"What?"

"You know, like your aunt." I didn't have any idea what he meant and decided he was looney. "Your aunt," he repeated. "A-N-T." He burst out laughing as the teachers came into the lunchroom to let us know it was time to head back to class. "See you later, cleanup boy."

Amanda and Darryl stood up and faced me. "So, what did you decide?" she asked. Darryl crossed his arms and stared at me without an expression.

I didn't know what she meant at first but then remembered she had wanted me to go to a movie with them tomorrow. I wanted to go, but it wasn't possible. It went against everything my mom had taught me.

Mr. Spradley walked back into the lunchroom with clean, damp pants. "I can't believe that happened," he complained to the janitor. "These kids…" He stared at me and shook his head.

"Want some spaghetti?" the janitor asked him.

I shrugged at Amanda and said, "I don't think I can go. Sorry." As I walked away with the other kids, all I could think about was how badly I wanted to miss just one day of school and hang out with the cool kids.

TWO

PLAYING DODGEBALL
WITH A JAGUAR

As soon as I walked into my computer class, Miss Causey caught my attention. "Jake, come here for a minute." The odd thing about her was she was super short and big, and her boyfriend, the school resource officer, was super tall and thin. "Why were you sent to the front of the cafeteria?" she asked, concerned.

I wasn't sure she'd believe me if I told her about the flying tray, or even if I believed it myself, so I summarized it as best as I could. "I sat at a different table today." I looked to the back of the room where Darryl was. "Not everyone liked that."

She put a hand over her chest and blew out a breath of air like she was relieved to hear I hadn't robbed the lunch ladies. "I knew you couldn't do anything bad. You're the best student I've ever had. I'd clone you a hundred times if I could."

I wondered if a hundred clones of me would wear the same clothes and eat the same food. Eh, who cares? I wondered if one of them could be cool and do something bad. I was tired of being good all the time and making adults happy while other kids mocked me.

"I can be bad," I whispered. Miss Causey must have heard me because she chuckled like it was absurd. I put my head down and headed to my seat while kids jeered at me for making them sit through silent lunch.

"Be careful," Tony warned the class. "He might get angry and do extra homework!" The whole class laughed until Amanda stood up and told them to leave me alone.

I thanked her and took the empty seat next to her that belonged to Omar. One of my regular lunchroom buddies had told me in the halls that Omar had gone to the nurse's station then was sent home with the flu. If I had to guess, he had the mashed potatoes and gravy flu (and maybe Mr. Spradley had it now too!).

"Don't listen to him," Amanda advised me. "He's always got a bad attitude."

"Then why do you hang out with him?" I asked.

She opened her mouth to say something but was

interrupted by Jennifer, another popular girl, as she walked by.

"Hey, Amanda." Jennifer glanced at me and rolled her eyes. "You don't have to sit next to him," she said in a strong whisper, like I wasn't supposed to hear it but she meant for me to anyway. "There's an empty seat by me."

I sank in my chair.

"I'd rather sit by my friend," Amanda responded.

Jennifer rolled her eyes at me again and stomped off to her desk.

"You didn't have to do that," I told Amanda.

"I wanted to." She smiled softly.

I smiled back because she made me feel important. I was still hurt by what Jennifer had said though. I guess it didn't matter who I hung out with, I still wouldn't be cool to the rest of the world. "I wish I was popular like you," I mumbled.

Amanda chuckled. "It's not as great as you think it is." She looked down at her desk and sighed. "I wish I could go back in time and change everything."

I was shocked to hear her say that because her life seemed great to me. I didn't know her very well, but it seemed like everyone wanted to be her friend and would do whatever she asked them to do.

If I could go back in time, I'd go all the way back to kindergarten and start being cool. I'd learn every sport and practice them every day until I became really good at them. I'd hang out with the kids I knew were going to be cool one day, so I'd be cool by association.

"I didn't mean to get you in trouble earlier," Amanda assured me. "Darryl is very protective and—" She clutched her chest like she was having a heart attack then pulled up on the necklace that was tucked beneath her shirt. At the bottom of it was an emerald that glowed bright green. "Oh, no."

"What?" I asked as she tucked the emerald quickly back under her shirt so no one could see it. The gem was beautifully spectacular, something I'd show the whole world if I had it, not hide it away. The light in Amanda's eyes was gone, and her face was drawn as if she had received the worst possible news.

The fire alarm suddenly screamed its deafening roar. Orange and red lights flashed around the room.

"Everyone up!" Miss Causey shouted over the fire alarm. "Line up in an orderly fashion and let's head to the courtyard." We had practiced this drill twice every month during the school year, but no one said it was going to happen today. Maybe there really was a fire this time, but I suspected whatever was wrong had something to do with Amanda's glowing emerald.

Before I could stand up, Darryl appeared behind Amanda and threw a coat over her head as he led her out of the room urgently. Tony tagged along right behind them and knocked me down before I could get out of my seat. I had to catch up with them to find out what was going on.

By the time I got up and reached the door, the hall was flooded with kids from classes all over the school. Amanda and the new kids were nowhere in sight. What was Amanda being protected from?

I fought through the crowd until I finally spotted them separating themselves from everyone else and slipping into the gym. I squeezed and pushed through as many kids as I could until I reached the gym and slipped in just like the cool new kids.

The gym was empty. Basketball hoops stood at

both ends of the floor and empty bleachers sat on both sides. I had seen Amanda and the others come in here, so I knew they had to be close. Maybe they were in a locker room behind the basketball nets. I decided to check the boys' room first because, well, it'd be too weird being caught in the girls' locker room.

Just as I stepped into the room, I heard Amanda scream from somewhere behind the gym. I raced to the rear door that led to the outside track and pulled the door open hastily.

I froze in disbelief when I saw what was outside in front of me.

The largest cat I had ever seen bared its sharp, powerful fangs and roared at Amanda, Darryl, and Tony. The cat's coat was yellow and orange with black spots like a jaguar but that was crazy—jaguars didn't live anywhere near here.

Darryl stood in front of Amanda to protect her with his hands out in defense. Tony was running away across the track like an all-star athlete.

I'm not sure why, but I had an overwhelming desire to protect Amanda. No one outside seemed to realize I was standing in the doorframe, watching them in suspense. I grabbed the only weapon I could find close by—a dodgeball.

I threw the dodgeball as hard as I could at the jaguar, who was in my direct path. I'd like to say the jaguar fell over then ran away when the ball hit it, but honestly, the ball never made it there. It hit the ground before it reached the jaguar and bounced right over the monstrous cat.

That's when I faced the scariest moment of my life (at that time).

The jaguar swiveled its head toward me and smiled with its fangs dripping hot saliva. I'm not kidding. The cat smiled like it was happy to see me, like I was the one it wanted to tear apart. It roared again and sprinted toward me like a freight train.

I froze. They say your life flashes before your eyes right before you die. That's a lie. It's more like everything moves in slow motion. I could see and hear every footfall of the jaguar as it barreled toward me. I watched Amanda's mouth open wide and her arms wave back and forth in what seemed to take minutes instead of seconds.

"Jake!" I finally heard Amanda's voice shout. "Run!"

I turned around and forced my feet to move faster than they had ever moved before across the gym floor. The jaguar roared behind me, its breath on my heels. My heart beat faster than any heart was meant to beat. My ears felt like they were on fire.

But I was going to get out. I was going to survive. I had to.

That's when my sneakers squeaked on the floor, and I tumbled onto my knees and arms and face. I instinctively huddled my limbs together like a baby in its mother's womb to protect myself. There was nothing else I could do but wait to be eaten alive.

I watched in slow motion as the jaguar jumped into the air to pounce on me. Its fangs were beautiful and huge as they came down toward my head.

The jaguar unexpectedly yelped, and its body rose up into the air like my lunch tray had then soared across the gym and slammed into the wall like it had been hit by a semi-truck.

I sat up as Darryl stood over me and kept an eye on the jaguar. It got back up slowly on its four paws and shook its head like it was trying to get water out of its ears. The big cat looked around the gym at me and Darryl like it had never seen us before. It seemed confused about where it was and how it got there. After searching for a way out, it walked cautiously through the open back door.

Darryl reached out a hand to me and helped me up. He nodded like he respected me now. "It's not your job to protect her," he advised me. He stepped to the side to show Amanda behind him. "It's mine." He guided her out the way they had gone before.

"Are you okay?" Amanda shouted back at me.

Darryl kept guiding her. "Is he okay?" she asked him.

The janitor stood at the gym entrance with his mouth wide open, apparently having seen me run through the gym. "Dude, that was awesome. You were almost cat food."

I didn't say anything to him. I wasn't sure I could or even if I could ever move from that spot again. Every cell in my body felt numb.

Tony walked in and shook his head at me. "A dodgeball? Really?" He walked away slowly backward and snapped his fingers. "Tomorrow. Forget about school. We're gonna blow your mind!"

THREE

THE DOOR
WITH ORANGE LIGHT

"Jake, are you listening to me?" my mom asked, sitting across from me at the dining room table at home that night. "How was your day?" She twirled spaghetti noodles around her fork and shoved them down her throat. My stomach made weird noises, like my throat did when I gargled mouthwash. I could never eat spaghetti again after what the school janitor had said.

"I spilled milk all over myself," I told her in a daze. I stared at the wall. My mind refused to process what had happened at school.

My stepdad John pulled a small bottle of hand sanitizer out of his pocket, popped open the lid, and squeezed a big gob of gel into one palm. He slammed the bottle on the table and rubbed the gel between his hands vigorously. He had a bushy mustache like a cop from the '80s and wore a silk shirt that had gone out of style long before I was born. He was at the head of the table. "Are those the clothes you wore to school? Please tell me you changed your clothes."

John is what you would call a germophobe. He was a nice enough guy, but he thought every little germ would make him sick or eat the skin off his body. He made my mom happy, so I had learned to ignore it. "Yep. No germs here."

"Jake, honey, are you okay?" my mom pressed. "You haven't touched your food, and you won't stop looking at the wall." She always knew when something was wrong with me. I wished I could tell her everything.

"Milk can have salmonella, e. coli, listeria…" John said in a trance, rocking slightly back and forth.

"Hush," my mom said to him. "You don't have to scare everyone." She was less than five feet tall but was a fighter. Everyone knew her as the sweetest lady in the world. They didn't know that she carried a handgun by her ankle and practiced at the shooting range five days a week, like she was preparing for something dangerous that was coming.

My stepdad's face turned red, and I knew there

was going to be another argument about how dangerous germs were. I had to stop it.

"The vice principal made me stand with the bad kids at lunch today," I blurted.

John stopped rocking back and forth.

"What?" my mom asked, her face twisted in confusion. "I'm going down to the school first thing in the morning with you to make this right."

"I'm not going to school tomorrow," I told her, still staring at the wall. I had decided that it was time to finally break the rules and find out more about the cool new kids.

My mom put her hand on my forehead. "It's warm. Are you feeling sick?"

"Omar Kim went home with the flu." I'm not sure why I said it, but I did.

"The flu?" my stepdad asked, horrified. He stood up from his chair and backed away from the table. "I have to go out of town for a conference tomorrow. I can't get sick. I can't."

I had never lied to my mom before, and I felt bad, really bad. "I'm not sick," I admitted as she ran into the kitchen to make me some chicken soup.

"I'll call Dr. Wright in the morning," she said,

not hearing what I had told her over the refrigerator's hum. "I'm the only worker at the daycare until noon. Charlotte is on vacation." She didn't wear the gun while at the daycare—they didn't let her. She walked in circles, trying to figure out what to do. "Are you okay by yourself for a few hours in the morning? I'll make the appointment in the afternoon."

"Hey," John said to me as he stood and peeked into the kitchen to make sure my mom couldn't hear him. "I don't really have a conference tomorrow."

"What?"

"Yeah, there's no conference." He peeked into the kitchen again and smiled. "Tomorrow is our six-month anniversary and I'm gonna surprise your mom."

I couldn't believe it had been six months since they got married. And who celebrated six-month anniversaries? We celebrated birthdays once a year. Christmas once a year. Even summer break was only once a year.

"I'm gonna be at your mom's job with a horse carriage full of roses when she gets there tomorrow morning. We'll ride through the farms in town and stop to pick berries." He paused and smirked. "Charlotte isn't on vacation." He had a huge smile on his face like he was proud of himself for setting it all up and excited about how happy my mom was going to be. And it was true, she loved horse carriages.

"White carnations," I said. He raised his eyebrows. "She likes white carnations."

He nodded at me. "Thanks. You're a good kid."

"Listen, John," I said, feeling bad, "I've got to be honest with you. I'm not going to—" It occurred to me just then that a horse carriage wouldn't be great for him. "My mom will love what you're doing, but aren't you afraid of the germs?"

He sighed and said, "A man's gotta do what a man's gotta—" His cellphone chirped a Mariah Carey song. He answered it and assured the other person as loudly as he could that he'd be on the first plane out of town so he could be at the conference tomorrow. He lowered the phone and put his hand over the speaker as he got up and stood in front of the kitchen. "I have to take this," he said to my mom. "Please bleach everything in the house before you come to bed. I can't get sick. I can't." He winked at me as he rushed off and smothered his hands in sanitizer again.

My mom came back to the table and sat down. "The soup will be ready in a few minutes."

"Mom, listen to me," I said to her, making sure I had her undivided attention. "I'm going to skip school tomorrow. Not because I'm sick. I'll probably be in a lot of trouble." I waited for her to yell at me after her expression dropped and maybe ground me for a month.

But that's not what happened.

Her frown slowly turned into a smile and then a laugh. "You were always the funny one in the family. Great joke!"

I gave up and put my head on the table as my dog, a feisty Chihuahua named Blondie, whimpered at my feet. I flicked a meatball off my plate and right into her ravenous mouth.

"Nothing cures sickness faster than laughter," my mom said. "Remember when you were younger, and we drove under bridges?" She spread her arms in a wide arc over her head. "You would shout, 'Duck!' so we'd all bend over and not get our heads chopped off." She smiled and snorted.

All I could do was shake my head at the ridiculousness of it. You're inside the car—a bridge can't chop your head off.

My mom stood up and walked around the table to stand by my side. She put her arm in front of my face and swept it slowly over my head. "Bridge!" she shouted.

I didn't move. It wasn't a bridge.

"Jake, your head got chopped off," she cried out.

"Oh, no." She put her arm in front of me again and swept it slowly over my head. "Bridge!"

I smiled and shook my head.

My mom refused to give up and put her arm in front of me again. She moved it much slower this time. "Here comes the bridge, Jake. Here it comes. Get ready... Bridge!"

She won. I caved in and shouted, "Duck!" We both leaned over the table and couldn't stop laughing.

"See? Don't you feel better?" she asked. She put her hand on my head and messed up my hair before rushing back into the kitchen. "Let me find you some medicine. We'll have you back to normal in no time."

I loved my mom but hated that she didn't think I could do anything wrong. No one did. But worse than that, I didn't think my life would ever get back to normal after that day.

*****

I had a hard time falling asleep that night because the whole house smelled like bleach. I tossed and turned, thinking about that jaguar attacking me. Where did it come from? Why was it there? Did it actually recognize me or did I imagine it? Why did it want to eat me?

Then came the questions about the cool new kids. Who were they really? Why were they interested in me? Why did I want to protect Amanda so badly? How did Darryl make things fly?

Toss and turn. Toss and turn. I couldn't get comfortable. Nothing made sense, and my mind wouldn't stop racing.

Sleep finally came and the world turned dark but only for a few seconds before I started dreaming. In my dream, I faced the same door I had faced every night since I could remember. It was a monstrous wooden door, standing tall and alone in a field of colorful wildflowers.

As I approached it, I recalled the thousands of times I had tried to open it, but it wouldn't budge. I tried again. With every turn of my hand on the knob, a stream of glowing orange light burst through slits in the door.

I banged on it in frustration.

Something was different this time though. It didn't feel like a dream because the door was more real than it had ever been before. I could feel the cold metal of the knob and the warm wind blowing on my back. I could smell the dampness of the wood and the fragrant wildflowers all around me.

The door was there for me to open, but it still wouldn't allow me in. What great secret was it hiding from me, and what did I have to do to open it?

"You have to believe," a strangely familiar voice called out.

I turned to my side and gasped. It was Amanda.

FOUR

MY FRIENDS HAVE VANISHED

I woke to what sounded like a car horn honking at seven o'clock the next morning. I sat up, yawned, and stretched my arms over my head when I noticed a folded piece of paper in my lap. I opened it up to find a twenty-dollar bill and these words:

Jake, I'll be home around noon. You have an appointment with Dr. Wright at two o'clock. There's more cold and flu medicine on the kitchen counter. Here's $20 if you want to order some food, but I left some chicken soup in the fridge for you. Call me if you need anything. Love, Mom

I couldn't believe my luck! I wasn't going to school and I'd have a doctor's note excusing me for the day. I was going to see the movie I'd been dying to see with the cool new kids and…

Wait.

They never asked for my phone number, and I didn't tell them where I lived. I crumpled up the paper and threw it across the room. I didn't have any contact with Amanda, Darryl, or Tony so it looked like I was going to sit there for the next four hours then go to the doctor when I wasn't even sick.

It wasn't fair!

The same car horn that had woken me up honked again but longer this time. I got up and opened my bedroom blinds to see who couldn't keep their sticky fingers off the steering wheel.

I smiled and scratched my head when I saw Amanda leaning against what looked like a bright red classic Ford Mustang from the '50s or '60s—so awesome! How did she know I lived here? She smiled back and waved for me to come join her. Darryl was in the front passenger seat with a scowl on his face. Tony was in the driver's seat, saluting me and honking the horn over and over again.

I held up a finger to let them know I'd be a minute then raced to throw some clothes on, brush my teeth, and slather deodorant over my armpits. I didn't know how they found me, and I didn't care. I was so excited that I was going to be a part of their gang for a day and learn more about them!

I snatched the twenty bucks off my bed and raced

out the door. As I was locking it, I paused, wondering if I was doing the right thing. Well, I knew I wasn't doing the right thing. I could still be the person that every adult wanted me to be. All I had to do was go back inside, make my mom understand the truth when she got home, get detention, then get shipped off to some school in another country.

Blondie appeared at the opposite side of the living room window by the door, scratching at the glass and whimpering. I had never seen her jump around so much as she barked wildly, like she was warning me not to go.

Amanda shrieked right before her car door slammed shut.

I jumped when the horn honked as I turned around to see what had scared her. "Here goes nothing." I took a deep breath and walked to the beautiful red car.

Darryl opened the driver's door and said to Tony, "Get out of my seat." I was surprised there wasn't an adult with us and wondered if it was safe for Darryl to drive. We were all in the sixth grade, but I suspected he was older than us, maybe sixteen.

"Why'd you bring that?" Amanda asked as I sat in the backseat with her. She pointed at the backpack in my hands that I hadn't even realized I had brought along.

"Habit, I guess," I said. "It's a school day."

"What changed your mind?" she asked as we pulled out of the driveway and onto the empty road.

I shrugged. "You guys are cool. I want to be a part of that." *And I want to know how Darryl can make things fly and why the boys are protecting you.* "And I have to prove to myself that I don't always have to be good."

Amanda scoffed. "You are good, Jake. Don't ever lose that."

"So, um, why did you scream outside?" I asked, trying to change the subject.

She looked out her window. "Your dog scared me." I'm not sure how Blondie could scare anyone because she weighed less than five pounds. All she did to people was lick them.

The car radio squealed and then two men were talking on a morning show.

"Bobo the spider monkey has escaped from the county zoo," one of them reported. "Hide your bananas!"

"How does a monkey escape from the zoo?" the other asked, seeming surprised. "It's like Alcatraz in there."

"Alcatraz was a prison surrounded by water," the first guy said like everyone knew that. "The zoo isn't."

"Maybe the zoo should move to Alcatraz so monkeys can't escape," the second guy said smugly.

"Seriously, though, folks, if you see the monkey, do not approach it because it could be dangerous," the first guy advised. "Call wildlife officials immediately."

"I always wanted a squirrel monkey that I could walk around town with on my shoulders," I said to Amanda.

"Why?" she asked.

I shrugged. "It's silly." I had studied all kinds of monkeys, like spider monkeys and squirrel monkeys, for years in hopes I could convince my mom to get me one but, yeah, that didn't work out. I love every animal because they seem to understand me more than people.

"He shouldn't be here," Darryl muttered from

the front seat while looking at me in the rearview mirror.

"Drive faster," Amanda complained to Darryl. "I don't want to miss the previews."

*****

The ticket salesman at the movie theater stared at me when I asked for a ticket to see *Party Marty*. It was only rated PG, but I'm sure he knew I was supposed to be in school but was skipping out like troublemakers do. I even had my backpack slung over one shoulder out of habit. He shook his head and said, "Right on," as he took my money and handed me a ticket.

Darryl was behind me and asked for two tickets as he stepped up, one for him and one for Amanda. The salesman didn't hesitate and gave the tickets right to him after he paid. I wondered if Darryl's facial hair made him look like a man to other people. Maybe I'd grow a beard myself.

Tony paid quickly and asked Darryl to wait for him. "I need to talk to you," he said in a serious tone.

"Can it wait?" Darryl asked. "The movie's about

to start."

"What I have to say isn't for all ears," Tony assured him, nodding in my direction like I was the enemy.

Darryl sighed and asked Amanda to go inside with me so she wouldn't miss the previews she wanted to see so badly. She looked from him to me with her hands in front of her like she was unsure. "I'll be right here," he comforted her. "You'll be safe with Jake."

She agreed and waved for me to follow her inside until we reached the right room just as the lights started going dark. She led us to center seats in the middle row so we'd have the best overall view.

I thought it was odd when Amanda asked me to leave an empty seat between us so Darryl could sit there and Tony on the other side of her. Why was she so reliant on them always being close to her? It's not like I bite.

I sat back as the first preview began to play on the big screen. All I wanted to do was enjoy the movie then get back home in time before my mom took me to the doctor. The cool new kids wanted the same thing, so I was sure I wouldn't learn much about them that day. I just had to keep my head low and stay out of trouble.

A group of five loud, obnoxious college guys barged into the theater, talking and laughing all the way to the seats right in front of us.

"The car's almost out of gas, man," one of them complained. "We'll be lucky to make it out of the parking lot." He grabbed a handful of popcorn out of a theater bucket and tossed it at one of his friends. Popped kernels flew onto my head and into my lap.

"Stop complaining!" the friend replied as he threw his own handful of popcorn back at the other guy. "Be happy I brought your sorry butt."

Amanda didn't seem to notice they were even there as she kept looking back at the entrance to the room, waiting for Darryl to walk through it. When the previews ended and the movie started, she stood and came to my side. "We need to check on the others."

"The movie just started," I complained. I had been waiting to see it for months and had risked my reputation to be there. I couldn't even miss five minutes of it because an important scene that revealed the whole plot of the movie could happen.

"Please, Jake," she begged me. "I don't feel safe." I didn't understand why she didn't feel safe with me. Hadn't I proven myself with the jaguar? Well, sure, it almost ate me, but that wasn't the point.

"Fine," I told her as I reluctantly got up and walked through the dark room with her and back into the lobby. She hyperventilated when she saw that they weren't there. "They're probably still talking outside," I said, concerned but unsure.

Amanda opened the glass doors to get outside and we immediately noticed that Darryl and Tony weren't there either. "Something bad has happened," she warned me. "We're in danger."

She was being ridiculous because the most dangerous thing at the theater was popcorn flying into my face. "Maybe they snuck into another movie," I tried to convince her. "People do it all the time."

She shook her head and pointed at the parking lot. That's when I realized the bright red classic Ford Mustang was gone.

FIVE

ROTTEN APPLE
ROTTEN MONKEY

We stepped onto the hot asphalt and walked around the parking lot, searching for the car that had brought us to the theater. It was nowhere to be found. "Maybe they went to get some gas," I suggested to Amanda, "or put some air in the tires." I didn't believe either one of those was true, but I couldn't figure out why Darryl and Tony had abandoned us.

Amanda kept running her fingers through her hair and turning from side to side like she expected the boys to pop up and surprise her. "They're supposed to protect me," she whispered, almost in tears.

"Your boyfriend wouldn't leave you here," I assured her. "Even I wouldn't do that to you." I wondered if they were playing a practical joke on me by leaving me out of town on a school day.

"You wouldn't, would you?" she asked. She spun

slowly in a full circle, scanning the parking lot one last time. "Jake," she said, standing in front of me and looking into my eyes, "I swear on my life to protect you. Do you swear on your life to protect me?"

If anyone else had asked me that question, I would have thought they were crazy. While I felt a strong connection to her and an unexplainable desire to keep her safe, I couldn't help but remember how I had failed to stop the jaguar. "Your boyfriend should be back any minute."

She scoffed and said, "Is that what you think? You think Darryl's my boyfriend?"

"Well, yeah," I admitted. "Everyone thinks that. You're always together. He does everything for you."

"He's ... he's not my boyfriend," she said with a red face. "He's my cousin."

I banged a palm against my forehead. "Sorry. If you're in any trouble at all, I'll protect you as best as I can." *But there better not be any more jaguars!*

Amanda gasped and clutched her chest. She reached for the chain around her neck and lifted it up from beneath her shirt again, with the emerald glowing bright green.

"Oh, no," she cried. "This can't be happening. Not now." She spun around desperately with her chest heaving up and down.

"What are we looking for?" I asked, scanning the parking lot, afraid of what the answer might be. Then I heard the strangest sound from the trees around the parking lot. I knew the sound because I had heard it many times before at the zoo.

"No way!" I shouted when I spotted the source. "It's a monkey, the one we heard about on the radio." It dangled with long arms from two opposing tree limbs, whinnying playfully like a horse and watching us. The spider monkey's head was black, and its furry body was brown.

I took a step toward the monkey. I had always wanted to hold one and play with it. "This is so awesome."

"Don't go," Amanda said, reaching out a hand for me to come back.

"It looks harmless," I replied as the monkey whinnied again and swung toward me. "Maybe it needs a friend." I stepped closer and closer to the primate, exhilarated to be near it.

"It's not what you think," Amanda shouted. "It

embodies the evil prince," she said hesitantly, like I wasn't supposed to know that. She stood behind a car, using it as a shield from something.

What in the world was she talking about? She was cool but maybe a little crazy. Evil prince? I ignored her and walked right up to the monkey as it swung on the last branch before the parking lot.

The spider monkey stared at me and smiled—the most beautiful expression I had ever seen. I smiled back at it and made the same sounds it did so it knew it was safe with me. Then the monkey opened its mouth wide to bare its teeth and let out a high-pitched scream that nearly left me deaf.

I fell backward onto my hands and jumped right back up. My heart felt like a hammer beating against my chest. "Take cover!" I shouted back to Amanda as I looked into the monkey's angry face and cold eyes then turned back to the parking lot and ran. "I'll distract him!"

I ran toward the side of the parking lot opposite to the side Amanda was in as the monkey swung out of the trees and chased after me. There wasn't any reason to put both of us in danger. I couldn't figure out why Bobo the spider monkey had turned violent and wondered why it had escaped from the zoo.

I quickly pulled on the door handles of each car I passed, hoping one of the doors was unlocked and would open so I could jump inside and lock myself in. After five tries, I found one. I pulled the door open, dived inside, and slammed the door shut. I locked it tighter than a peanut butter jar.

The monkey banged on the door with powerful fists, leaving little dents all over it as the car rocked back and forth. I couldn't stop shaking. I covered my face and turned my back to the primate.

After what must have been minutes, the banging stopped.

I uncovered my face and turned back toward the window. The monkey stood there, smiling at me again like it wanted to be my friend. It was a beautiful, magnificent creature. It put one hand on the window to connect with me. I made myself believe it wanted peace and moved to place my hand on the opposite side of the window, like we were touching.

Before my hand reached the window, the monkey left only his index finger in the air. He waved the finger from side to side as if I had done something wrong and was about to be punished for it.

The monkey turned toward Amanda and screamed again before racing after her. I had promised to protect her with my life, and that's what I was going to do. I tried to open the car door, but the handle rocked back and forth like it was busted. I couldn't get out!

The monkey jumped on top of the car that Amanda was hiding behind and barked at her like a wild dog. I rolled my window down manually and opened the door from the outside then blasted toward Amanda.

I flung my backpack off and swung it at the monkey when I reached Amanda's side behind the car. The primate hissed at me and screamed. I huddled next to Amanda as she sat with her back to the car and her arms wrapped around her legs.

"Give me your bag!" she yelled at me. I had no idea why she wanted it but didn't argue. She snatched it from me and quickly unzipped the bookbag, pulled out my books one by one, and tossed them into the parking lot.

"Hey!" I protested.

The last thing she pulled out was an old lunch bag that I carried my snacks in. She emptied it in front of her and grabbed an apple I had already taken a huge bite out of that was turning brown around the teeth marks.

"This will work," she said as she stood and faced the monkey.

"Wait!" I yelled, knowing the monkey would attack her. My world fell into slow motion again. Amanda leaned back as the monkey swung a powerful arm at her. She held out the apple to the monkey and let it try to take the apple from her. The monkey reached out to take it but missed before she pulled her arm back as far as she could then tossed the apple into the trees.

The monkey looked from Amanda to me, seeming conflicted, then jumped off the car and ran after the apple.

I grabbed Amanda's hand and raced back to the car I had hidden in while the monkey was distracted. My world seemed to freeze when the theater doors opened and a mom with two young children stepped out. They looked to be maybe five years old.

"A monkey!" the girl yelled as she ran away from

her mom and toward the spider monkey. Her brother ran off with her. The mom yelled for them to come back and tried to catch up with them.

Amanda pulled on my hand and yelled for me to hurry up so we could get out of there. I pulled back on her hand.

"They're little kids," I told her. "We can't let them get hurt."

She pulled harder. "We have to stay alive. For my world and for yours. Please."

What she said didn't make any sense and I didn't have time to argue with her. I watched the monkey bite into the apple he had reached and stared back at the children running toward it, confused. Then the monkey smiled at me as the children got closer.

I squeezed my hand out of Amanda's.

"No!" she shouted. She glanced at the car then back at the children.

I ran as fast as I could toward the monkey and the kids. They couldn't get hurt because of me. I wouldn't let them.

I caught a glimpse of Amanda taking a stance then pushing her hands out forcefully into the air in the monkey's direction. A glowing green streak of light flew past me then surrounded the monkey, caging him. I stopped in my tracks and looked back at Amanda, amazed and confused by what she had done.

"Let's go!" she shouted at me as she got into the driver's seat of the car and closed it.

I got in on the passenger's side and watched as the mother from the theater pulled her two kids away from the caged monkey. They appeared to be safe.

"You weren't supposed to see that," Amanda said.

I wasn't exactly sure what I had seen. Things were more confusing now than ever. Darryl could make things fly and Amanda could shoot green bolts of lightning? None of that mattered just then. "How do we protect others from the monkey?"

She searched the front of the car for something specific. "In a few minutes, that monkey won't remember anything that happened here today."

"Like the jaguar," I realized, remembering how it had walked out of the gym in confusion. "But why?"

She took a deep breath and stared at me as she fidgeted with wires beneath the steering wheel. I noticed her emerald wasn't glowing anymore. "You don't understand. None of this will stop until the prince—"

The car started up.

"Yes!" Amanda exclaimed. That's when I realized she had hotwired it, something we definitely didn't learn in school. We wouldn't even be able to drive for another three years.

"How did you know how to do that?" I asked, impressed.

She winked at me. "Just lucky, I guess." The tires screeched as we barreled out of the parking lot.

SIX

BABY ALLIGATORS
LOVE HOT DOGS

We sat silently in the car as we headed back to our city. Amanda stared straight ahead, and I couldn't tell if she was focused on the road or avoiding a conversation with me. I didn't want to point out to her that she wasn't supposed to be driving a car yet. My mom would kill me if I ever did that.

"How did you know?" I asked her.

She blinked her eyes and cleared her throat. "What? What are you talking about?"

"Most people think monkeys only like bananas," I said. "How did you know it would like the apple?"

She shrugged. "I didn't." She kept staring at the road before us.

"They like all kinds of fruits and seeds," I explained. I decided that I'd keep an apple in my backpack every day from now on, just in case. And I decided that I didn't want a spider monkey as a pet. A squirrel monkey maybe. They weren't dangerous, right?

"You could've run," Amanda blurted. She turned her head to me for the first time. "Why didn't you?"

"I don't break my promises," I said, smiling at her.

"I'm sorry," she whispered, her face turning red.

"For what?" I wondered aloud.

"I wanted to run." She glanced at me and said, "But you're different. You stayed behind to protect those kids, even though you didn't have to."

"Neither did you," I reminded her. "You're the one who saved them."

She smiled and nodded as if she realized what she had done for the first time.

I pointed to the emerald she had left hanging over her shirt. It had been its normal shade of green ever since we got into the car. "How do you make that glow?"

She looked down at it and tapped her fingers on the steering wheel like she was thinking hard. She stopped tapping and held on tight. "It only glows when I'm in danger."

That sounded weird, but I thought about the times I had seen it light up. The emerald had glowed at school before the jaguar attacked and at the theater before the monkey attacked.

"You believe me, right?" she asked. "It's okay if you don't. It's probably better that way." Yeah, I believed her, but I wasn't sure what was real and what wasn't anymore. I mean, I had watched green bolts of lightning shoot out of her hands. Maybe I was going crazy.

The gas light flashed on the car dashboard to signal that we were almost out of gas and weren't going much further. "The college kids at the theater," I mumbled. I could still taste some of their popcorn on my lips.

"This is the car they were complaining about," Amanda realized. The car sputtered its last few breaths as she inched it into the closest parking lot. It led to a miniature golf course with live baby gators and large lifelike dinosaurs. A peaceful lake with ducks sat across the street.

*****

"I need to call my mom," I told Amanda, feeling sick to my stomach as she parked the car. "I'll see if they have a phone around here." I didn't have my own cell phone, but I knew when I was in too much trouble to handle things on my own and when to ask for help. Sure, I was going to be in a ton of trouble, but my mom always knew what to do. And I hoped John wouldn't be too mad at me for interrupting the horse carriage ride.

"Okay," Amanda agreed without hesitation. "I'll wait here." She kept looking out her window at the pond with dozens of baby gators staring back at her. A short fence kept them away from us.

I stepped out of the car and locked the door before closing it because too many weird things were happening when I was around Amanda and I didn't want anything dangerous to get into the car. I gave her a thumbs up to show her that we were safe. She smiled weakly and returned a thumbs up.

I passed by a tyrannosaurus, velociraptor, and an allosaurus that were all fake but looked very real and lifelike. They towered over me at fifteen feet tall and taller as I walked through them (shaking) and reached the front counter. A chubby man in a Hawaiian T-shirt looked back at me from behind the counter and nodded.

"How many?" he asked.

The only sport I was good at was playing video games. I couldn't even throw a dodgeball. Miniature golf was way out of my league. Not that it mattered because I was only there for one reason. "Can I use your phone?"

He scratched his head and looked back at a phone on the table behind him. "Sorry, kid. It's only for business."

I sighed and looked around the empty parking lot. The fake dinosaurs had rust on them like no one had touched them in years. I wondered if anyone actually came to this place or even knew it existed. "I need to call my mom. I don't have a way to get home."

The man grunted then reached back and grabbed the phone. "No international calls," he said as he handed it to me. "My mom will get mad."

As I dialed the number to my mom's cell phone, I wondered if the Hawaiian T-shirt guy still lived with his mom. He looked as old as my parents. Would that be me one day? Would I be working at a hidden miniature golf course with no customers, wearing a Hawaiian T-shirt, and still living with my mom? I kind of hoped so.

"Hello?" my mom answered on her phone.

"Hi, Mom. It's me," I replied.

"Is everything okay?" she asked.

"Not really," I answered. I took a deep breath and explained how I had ended up in Spring Rock so I could see a movie. I told her every detail except for the monkey. "And now I don't have a way to get home."

The phone went silent for what seemed like minutes.

"Mom?"

I felt her disappointment as she breathed heavily into the phone. "Let me figure this out," she said. "I'll be there within an hour. What's the address?"

I looked back at the guy behind the counter. "What's the address here?"

He shrugged. "It's called Dinosaur Golf. It's right off the main highway." He scratched his head again like he was confused and had never been here before. "Maybe she can Google it."

"Mom?" I said into the phone.

"I heard him. Give me an hour. Love you."

"Love you too."

I handed the phone back to the man I no longer wanted to be like and wondered if he had skipped a lot of school when he was my age. I noticed a sign on the counter that said, "Gator Food, $2."

I pulled two dollars out of my pocket and handed it to the guy. "They don't bite … do they?"

He put a small plastic bag full of chopped-up hot dogs on the table. "Only if you put your hand in their mouths." He handed me what looked like a stick to "go fishing" with. "Tie the hot dog pieces to the end of the string on that pole."

I headed back through the dinosaurs to the car, thinking about eating a hot dog myself. When I reached the car, I motioned for Amanda to come out and join me. She hesitated at first but banged on the door in frustration. I had forgotten that it was broken on the inside.

"Sorry about that," I said after I opened the door for her. "My mom is on her way."

"We shouldn't be this close to dangerous creatures," she warned, hugging her back to the car.

"They can't hurt us," I assured her. "They're in a gated pond and they're just babies." I held out my stick pole and tied a hot dog wedge to the end of it.

"Watch. We can feed them."

"Jake, don't," she pleaded as I approached the pond.

I paused and thought about it. "Your emerald isn't glowing. You said it glows when you're in danger. Come on, this will be fun."

She reluctantly joined me as I reached the stick pole over the short fence that separated us from the gators. Dozens of the little critters crawled out of the pond and fought for the hot dog piece. It was gone in less than two seconds.

I handed the pole to Amanda. "Here. You try."

She pushed it away from her. "No thanks."

"Don't you like any animals?" I asked. "How about dogs?" I grabbed the rest of the hot dog pieces out of the bag and tossed them to the gators who savagely tore them apart.

She shook her head. "I have bad experiences with animals."

I didn't know anything about her past, but based on what I'd seen over the last twenty-four hours, I agreed that her experiences were not only bad but absolutely terrifying. "You said something about an evil prince. What's that about?"

Amanda looked down at her emerald and nodded as if it was safe to talk about that. "There is a man on my planet named Prince Badood who will stop at nothing to capture me. He has imprisoned my people and my father."

I wanted to believe her after all that we had been through, but she sounded crazy. "If he's on another planet, why would he try so hard to capture you here, on planet Earth?"

She placed a hand on my shoulder, the same way my mom did when she wanted my attention. "I am Princess Amanda from Planet Amagrandus. My father is the king." She turned her head. "Prince Badood is not a rightful heir to the throne and will do everything he can to destroy the heirs of my father so he can rule unopposed."

"Wait, wait, wait," I insisted before she kept going. There's something I had to make sure I understood. "The guy's name is Prince Bad Dude?"

"Prince Badood," she corrected me.

I held up a hand. "That doesn't work for me. If he's trying to hurt you, then I have to call him Prince Bad Dude."

She chuckled and smiled. I accepted her for who

she was, even if she was a little cuckoo. I mean random animals attacking us and green bolts of lightning shooting from her hands sounded more normal than what she had just said. I was glad to have her as a friend and would protect her from anything that attacked, animal or alien.

"So, um, that was green lightning that shot out of your hands, wasn't it?" I asked, wondering if she really came from another planet and if everyone there could do that. "When you caged the monkey."

She shrugged as if it was nothing unusual. "Something like that. It's a force that I've always had. Everyone in my family is born with one special power."

"No way." Not only was she a cool kid, but she was a cool kid with a superpower. Real or not, I wished I had been born on her planet and in her family. "That's so awesome. Does it hurt when you use it?"

"No," she said, looking down at her hands, squeezing them open and closed. "It kind of tickles."

I turned and threw my hands out toward the dinosaurs, pretending to zap them with green lightning. "It didn't work," I said with a grin. "My zapper's broken." Amanda burst out laughing with me. After several minutes, when I finally caught my breath, I looked over the baby alligators. "Forget about Prince Bad Dude. Stick with me. As long as I'm around, nothing bad—"

The emerald on the chain around Amanda's neck glowed bright green again. She backed away from the gator pond and grabbed my arm.

"Maybe it's a coincidence," I said, even though I didn't believe in coincidences anymore. "The sun could be reflecting off your emerald."

The loudest and strongest roar I had ever heard bellowed behind us and nearly knocked us down.

SEVEN

DINOSAURS
HAVE BAD BREATH

The chubby man in the Hawaiian T-shirt ran past us with his arms waving wildly over his head. "Save yourselves!" he shouted. "Run for your lives!"

I turned and looked up to see the massive tyrannosaurus I had walked under earlier move its head from side to side. Every nerve in my body tingled as the dinosaur lifted its legs from the bolts holding it down. It stepped away from the inanimate velociraptor and allosaurus.

"This can't be real," I said to Amanda, blinking my eyes, trying to wish it away. The T-rex no longer looked like a metallic statue. Its body was black, and its eyes were surrounded by orange scaly skin. But that's not what stood out the most. Its razor-sharp, bone-crunching teeth could rip anything apart, or anyone.

Amanda grabbed my arm and tried to pull me away. "Jake," she said shakily, "we have to run. We have to try."

I knew better than to try running from the monster that could run twelve miles an hour. I had learned plenty about T-rexes, going all the way back to pre-school. The beasts had great vision, an amazing sense of smell, and better hearing than my dog. "Don't move," I warned Amanda. "Don't make a sound."

Her emerald seemed to glow brighter than the sun at that very moment.

The T-rex pointed its humongous nose and jaw at us and roared again.

I held tight to Amanda's hand when she screamed and pulled her toward the street. "Now, run!"

The ground shook like an unforgiving earthquake as the monster lumbered after us. I was sure a crack would open in the road and swallow us alive. The car we had arrived in was smashed flatter than a piece of paper as the T-rex trounced over it.

Drivers slammed on their brakes as we raced onto the busy highway. One guy held down his car horn as we passed him like he was angry at us for making him stop.

"Sorry," I shouted at him. "Sorry!" Amanda jerked me forward as if I had no reason to apologize to the man holding his horn down. I couldn't argue because our time would be better spent escaping from the dinosaur.

That's when the T-rex stepped on the man's car hood, decimating it, and roared through the windshield at him. That was our chance, our only shot to get out of there. Another driver waved us over as we passed her and told us to get into her car. She was frantic, and I knew she would drive us out of there and to safety. There was no way for us to outrun the supreme hunter.

"Go," I said to Amanda. I looked back at the monster roaring at the man in the car. "I'll distract the T-rex." There was no reason for both of us to be eaten alive and I couldn't leave anyone else in danger.

Amanda waved away the lady who was trying to help. "I'm not running away anymore. We do this together," she told me. "Prince Badood controls the T-rex and won't stop until I am no more." Maybe she wasn't crazy after all. Dinosaurs didn't just pop up in modern times.

"I've had enough of Prince Bad Dude," I said. "Can you use your green lightning thingy to cage the T-rex like the monkey?"

She shook her head. "It's way too big."

I watched the T-rex lift its head and roar in slow motion. Why did I keep seeing things move in slow motion? What was wrong with me? "I've got to tell you something," I said to Amanda.

"What?" she asked, staring at the dinosaur with her mouth wide open.

"I think I'm cursed."

She turned her eyes to me. "Huh?"

"When the jaguar attacked me, I saw it running slow. Like really slow." Her expression didn't change. "And then when the monkey attacked us, I saw it swing at you in slow motion. And now the T-rex…"

"It's moving slowly," Amanda finished. She put a hand on my arm. "There's nothing wrong with you. You've been given a gift."

I chuckled. "A gift?" It was a sickness, like being dizzy while the world spins around your head. It couldn't be a gift.

"Yes," she said. "Think about it. When you're in

danger, you have time to make choices that no one else does." She paused and took her arm off me. "Why didn't I see this before? You're a time sorter."

"What are you talking about?"

Metal creaked when the T-rex stepped off the car and stared at me. It wasn't moving slowly anymore. Then it did something creepy and familiar. The dinosaur smiled at me with enormous, rusty teeth.

"Um, uh," Amanda stammered. "You can control time like a flip book. You can move every page faster or slower until you get to the end. It can be one object or everything around you. You just have to learn how to control it with your breathing."

The T-rex roared and slid its feet backward on the gravel then leaned forward like a bull about to attack.

"How does Bad Dude know where we are all the time?" I wondered aloud as my heart raced. I glanced at Amanda's emerald and had an idea. "Do you trust me?" I asked her frantically.

"Yes," she answered. "You've kept your promise to protect me."

"Give me your emerald."

She grabbed the chain around her neck and furrowed her eyebrows. "What?"

I held out my hand. "There's not enough time to explain." She hesitantly took the necklace off and handed it to me. I grabbed it and ran as fast as my legs allowed to the grass on the side of road facing the lake, far away from her.

"Hey!" I shouted at the T-rex. "Over here!"

"No!" Amanda shouted.

I took a deep breath and concentrated on the T-rex moving slower. Everything around me moved in slow motion again. The dinosaur ran at full speed toward me but seemed slower than a turtle as gravel flew up behind it like tiny, lazy balloons. I cocked my arm back and threw the emerald as far as I could over the water. I wondered if my adrenaline was super high as the emerald soared across the lake and landed in the middle of it before sinking.

The T-rex didn't pay any attention to Amanda as it blew past her and headed straight for me at normal speed. Why couldn't I keep time moving slower? Was it the end of the flip book? I closed my eyes while the ground vibrated all around me, wondering if this was the end.

The T-rex roared one last time as it ran past me and into the lake. I reopened my eyes and watched the dinosaur swim in circles around the lake, searching for the emerald. I remembered that T-rexes were strong swimmers.

"I don't understand," Amanda said as she rejoined me. "Why isn't it coming after us?"

"The emerald was never meant to warn you," I advised her. I was glad I was right about that because there had only been a fifty percent chance my suspicions were true. I had almost been dinosaur dinner. "It's a beacon so Prince Bad Dude can find you." But I didn't understand why the T-rex had ignored Amanda completely to get to the emerald, even as it ran right by her.

She stared at me and said, "That's impossible."

"Why?" I asked. "I've recently discovered that nothing is impossible."

She blinked her eyes and rubbed her forehead like she had a headache. "Because—"

We both jumped when my mom pulled up next to us in her car and honked her horn.

EIGHT

IT ALL MAKES SENSE
(NOT REALLY)

I sat quietly in the backseat of my mom's car with Amanda as my mom watched us through the rearview mirror. Her eyes were transfixed on Amanda's face. I was shocked and confused that my mom didn't seem angry about me skipping school and leaving town.

"Who's your new friend, Jake?" she asked.

"Um, uh, this is Amanda."

My mom smiled into the mirror and said, "Hello, Amanda. I love your green eyes." She turned her eyes away and focused on the road as we drove away. "Reminds me of a sweet little girl I used to know," she said quietly.

Amanda blushed. "Thank you." My mom didn't respond to her, seeming lost in her thoughts. Amanda leaned over to me and whispered, "Those people back there, they're in danger."

I had thought about that before getting into the

car, leaving the dinosaur swimming in circles on a futile hunt. "Prince Bad Dude will abandon the T-rex when he figures out you're no longer wearing the emerald." *Unless he drowns first!*

Amanda nodded, appearing confident. "Where is Darryl?" she mumbled, her face riddled with concern. "He would never leave me behind." She looked directly into my eyes. "The emerald ... long before we came to your planet, more than a hundred years ago, it was created to warn my family of danger."

I realized right away that her family had been in danger for a very long time, not from outside enemies but from whoever had created the emerald. "Who gave your family the emerald?"

Amanda put a hand on her stomach as if she felt sick. "Servants loyal to my family for hundreds of years." She shook her head like it didn't make any sense. "Tony's family."

I didn't know why Tony's ancestors had anything to do with this. I wondered if he knew about their deception.

The only thing I knew for sure was that I would give up everything to protect Amanda, a girl I had met only the day before. A princess from another planet. But I had to understand more. "Why did you come here to find me?" I asked, realizing it wasn't a coincidence that a princess came here from another planet and welcomed me into her group. "I'm nobody."

She took her hand off her stomach and put it over my hand. "You're more important than you realize."

"Wait a minute," I said, leaning away from her. "The emerald was created over a hundred years ago? Exactly how old are you?" I knew I wasn't whispering anymore when my mom cleared her throat.

"That's not polite, Jake," she admonished me, staring back through the rearview mirror again. "You never ask a lady her age or her weight." She winked at Amanda as she pulled into a shopping plaza that only had two stores open. One was a pet shop and the other was a small grocery store. "I wasn't expecting to drive this far today. I need to use the restroom."

Amanda unbuckled her seatbelt and scooted close to me as we drove slowly by the pet shop windows. Her skin was shaking against mine. I swallowed hard and stopped breathing as dogs, cats, hamsters, birds, rabbits, snakes, and fish became visible. An enormous tortoise sat inside the front door, looking out at us.

"Which store do you think will let me use their restroom?" my mom asked, looking back and forth at the two.

"The grocery store!" Amanda and I shouted at the same time. I loved animals, but I didn't want to be around any of them for the rest of the day.

My mom parked the car, made sure no one else needed to use the restroom, and then rushed out of the car and into the grocery store.

I took my seatbelt off and turned to Amanda. "I can control time. How crazy is that? I always wanted to control time. How did you know?"

She shrugged. "You're special, Jake. I have nothing to do with it."

I couldn't go back in time to become cool, but I could make time move slower and faster. What could be cooler than that? "Am I the only one? The only time sorter?"

She turned her head away and covered her eyes. "There is one other." She cleared her throat before turning back to me. "Prince Badood is growing stronger," she warned, no longer whispering. "I've never seen him control an animal that large."

I wanted to keep talking about my ability to control time, but she had changed the subject for some reason. Maybe it wasn't unusual on her planet, but here, on Earth, it was so far outside the realm of normal that I couldn't stop thinking about what I could do with it.

I took a deep breath. "The T-rex," I confirmed, though it wasn't really an animal. It had been a statue first. As I had suspected, it hadn't bothered going after her when I had the emerald, but I didn't know why. Something else was bugging me. "The jaguar, the monkey, the T-rex—they all lost control or ran away at the last minute."

"Prince Badood cannot get to me on this planet. He's transferring his mind into theirs." She raised her hands to her head and pressed an index finger on both sides. "But two minds in one body will fight for control."

"Multiple personalities," I mumbled, wondering what kind of technology her planet had to be able to transfer minds from one world to another. "But the dinosaur was a statue. It couldn't have a mind of its own."

"Inanimate objects have their own energy, their own personalities," she explained. "Prince Badood was able to match the vibrations of his energy with the dinosaur statue."

"Oh, okay," I said, even though I didn't completely understand and couldn't focus on what she had said. I watched through the windshield as a vulture dove out of the sky and landed on top of a dumpster at the end of the parking lot.

"Let's hope he's never strong enough to control a human mind," she said, her eyes in a trance. "If he did, who could we trust?"

This was getting weirder and weirder for me. I would have been willing to accept that the animals had attacked us because of an outbreak of rabies. "Why doesn't he come here himself or send alien soldiers after us?"

Two more vultures swooped down and surrounded the dumpster. One faced the car and stared directly at me. I wiped away a bead of sweat on my forehead and tried to remain calm as Amanda spoke.

"I came here with Darryl and Tony on my planet's last working ship, a ship meant to save the royal family. I wasn't supposed to, but I had to." She smiled weakly at me. "There's only one other way. My father came to this planet before, years ago, searching for a world safe enough to protect our people. He used a special door built for my family generations ago, allowing him to travel through space and time." She sighed and put her head down. "My father has been imprisoned by Prince Badood for years and no longer has access to the door."

I froze as I thought about the dream I had every night of my life—the one with the door standing in a field of wildflowers. "Does this door have orange lights?"

She shrugged. "He never talked much about it, and I haven't seen it since I was a baby. I'm not sure it even exists anymore." She crossed her arms and leaned back. "I never trusted Tony. We've got to find Darryl and figure out what to do next."

I agreed with her, but I had to know one more thing first because she never answered me. "If you're from another planet, why did you hop on the royal ship and come here to find me?"

I sat up and studied the dumpster then searched the entire parking lot with my eyes. The vultures were gone. Had I imagined them?

"Are you okay?" Amanda asked. I nodded. She took a deep breath and bit her lower lip. "After my father was imprisoned, Darryl and Tony took me into hiding for years. We only came out when we discovered who you were."

The pet shop's front door opened, and a huge dog walked out on four massive paws, restrained on a short leash by a short man with a backward cap on his head. The dog had large, pointed ears and was covered in thin, gray hair but had white rings around its neck, chest, legs, and tail. If I hadn't known any better, I'd say it was a wolf. It appeared much stronger than the man as it yanked him forward with every step toward the car we were in.

"We're safe in the car, right?" Amanda asked, pressing against me as the dog got closer.

"Yeah," I said. "We're fine." *I hope!*

The dog barked viciously at us as it walked by the car with its owner in tow. "Quiet down!" the short man shouted. "Bad dog! Bad dog!"

I'm not sure why, but I laughed. Amanda looked

at me like I was crazy, but then she laughed too. In fact, we couldn't stop laughing. There was nothing for us to be afraid of because Prince Badood couldn't find us without that emerald. We were perfectly safe.

"See?" I told her. "Nothing can hurt us while we're in here."

The passenger door on my side of the car opened from the outside. A familiar face stuck his head inside the car. "There you are!" Tony said with a fake smile. "I've been looking all over for you." His smile disappeared. "Let's have some fun."

NINE

AN UGLY ALIEN INSIDE AND OUT

I opened my eyes and looked around at an unfamiliar room. *Where am I? How did I get here?* The walls were white and a fireplace with logs in front of it was on the opposite side of the room. A large wooden rifle cabinet sat against the far wall, filled with guns visible through the glass doors. In front of me and all around the room stood the most magnificent creatures I had ever seen.

This room belonged to a trophy hunter. It was filled with a stuffed buffalo, rhinoceros, lion, and brown bear—all standing in super creepy poses like they were ready to attack. I had seen similar animals the year before on a fifth-grade field trip to the National Museum of Natural History and had been amazed by their breathtaking size and power. Not this time though. I gulped.

I turned to my right, and next to me was Darryl, sitting in a chair with his head hanging down. He appeared to be either asleep or unconscious. His arms were wrapped behind the chair, likely with his hands tied by rope. I attempted to reach out a hand and shake him to find out what was going on. That's when I realized I couldn't move. My hands were also tied behind my chair.

I tried to kick and worm my way out of the chair that held me captive until I ran out of breath and my face felt like it was on fire. *Who would do this? Tony? Why?* I caught a glimpse of another body on my left as I looked around for any way to escape.

"Mom?" I couldn't believe that she was also here, a prisoner to whatever fate awaited us. This wasn't right. She didn't deserve this. She was asleep like Darryl. I fought even harder against the rope and whatever else held me back. "Mom! Wake up!"

Her head lifted slowly, and her eyes opened. She swallowed hard like she was dehydrated. Her clothes were covered in dirt as if she had been tossed on the ground like a violent criminal. She looked over at me and said with tears, "Oh, no. No … no … no …. Did they hurt you?"

My mind was running a million miles an hour. *How did she get here? Is she hurt? How did Darryl get here? How did I get here? Where is Amanda? I've got to protect her!* "I'm okay," I assured my mom. "What did they do to you?"

She sighed in relief and shook her head. "There's not much time to explain. I need you to listen to me." I fidgeted in the chair, still trying to get out and get to her. "These people are not your friends, Jake. They only want to hurt us because of who we are."

I stopped fighting against my shackles. Amanda had wanted to tell me who I really was but didn't get the chance to. "Who are we?"

Darryl awoke and lifted his head. "Don't listen to her," he warned. He struggled to get out of his chair and grunted. "We have to work together to get out of here."

"We are the judges of Planet Amagrandus," my mom said. "They pretend to be our friends. They've come here to destroy our planet." I couldn't believe Amanda would do anything like that. It didn't make any sense. "Jake, honey, why do you think I go to the shooting range five days a week? It's our job to destroy them before they destroy us."

"Lies," Darryl whispered. "We came here to

protect you. You have to believe me. You have to believe Amanda." I wanted to believe him, I really did, but why would my mom make all of this up? And why did I have such a great desire to protect Amanda? I was so confused.

"Look at me," my mom demanded. "I'm your mother. I've never lied to you and I never will. We must destroy him and the others when we break free. It is our family's destiny to protect this planet."

I took a deep breath and cracked my neck before I turned back to Darryl. My mom had been training with her gun my entire life to protect us from something that threatened our existence. And she knew about Amagrandus … there's no way she could have known about that without someone telling her or having been there herself. "It's true. She never lies."

He stared at me and said something I'll never forget. "She's no longer your mother." I remembered what Amanda had said about Bad Dude's growing powers and wondered if it was possible.

"You're right," I said to my mom. "We have to get rid of him."

"That's a good boy," she replied with a big smile.

"You said this is our family's destiny," I reminded her. "John is part of our family now. He's going to help us, right?"

"Not this time," she said. "You know he's at a conference out of town."

I nodded slowly, having the answer I needed. It broke my heart because I could no longer trust my mom. "He's not at a conference. There is no conference. He went to your job earlier to surprise you for your anniversary. You're supposed to be in a horse carriage and picking berries." I shook my head. "But you weren't there, were you? You were already planning this moment."

Her smile disappeared. "You disappoint me, Jake." She pulled her hands from behind her back and stood up from her chair, having never been tied to it like Darryl and I were. She moved in front of me and looked down at my face. "You should always listen to your mother," she said in an older male's voice I had never heard. "You should have joined me. What a waste."

Now I knew for sure who I was talking to. "Prince Bad Dude." Amanda had been afraid that one day he would be able to control a human mind. I never thought it would be my mom's. He nodded at me in triumph, smirking through my mom's face. All I could do was laugh.

"I amuse you?" he asked.

"No," I told the prince controlling my mom's mind. "It's just that … I've been abducted by an ugly alien." Darryl chuckled. "Don't get me wrong. My mom's a pretty lady, but you're ugly inside and out."

Prince Bad Dude stepped back from me and clicked his tongue to make a tsk sound. "Princess Amanda will suffer greatly. I will destroy you and her precious protector Darryl now." He walked around the stuffed, hunted animals, admiring each one. He stopped in front of the brown bear with its arms outstretched to attack. "Such a beautiful creature." He stroked my mom's hand against the bear's cheek and let her body collapse to the floor, unconscious.

"Mom!" I shouted.

The bear came to life and let out a deafening growl.

TEN

NOW IT ALL MAKES SENSE (SORT OF)

The bear stood at least seven feet tall on its hind legs, baring sharp teeth in its wide-open mouth, dripping saliva all over the beige carpet. The beast ignored my mom's lifeless body and took a step toward Darryl and me, roaring like a bulldozer from halfway across the room.

"Darryl!" I called out. I could only think of one way for us to survive for another minute. "Back your chair up to mine!" If I could reach his hands from behind his chair and if he could reach mine, maybe there'd be enough time for us to untie the ropes holding us back.

The bear was getting closer every second. Sweat dripped off my forehead and crashed on the carpet as I used my legs to turn my chair to let the back of it face Darryl's. He scooted his chair up right behind me.

As I reached for his hands, I immediately realized

there was no rope, just his bare hands. I kept moving my fingers up past his wrists while I kept an eye on the bear, which would be upon us in no time. It was distracted by the other stuffed animals.

There! I found it! There wasn't any rope binding our hands. We were held captive by thin strips of plastic that I recognized as zip ties. My family had some at home to hold a bunch of wires together behind the TV.

"Darryl!" I shouted quickly. "Back away from me! It's zip ties!" I guessed he didn't know what that was, but he scooted away without question. He struggled though, still appearing weak and groggy after waking up. That gave me a few seconds to free myself the way I had seen on a news special once.

I pushed my bound hands away from my back and raised them as high as I could then I drove my hands toward me quickly, banging them against the back of the chair. Nothing changed, and my hands were still bound, but it hurt my wrists more than the time I broke my baby toe playing soccer.

The bear roared again after it pushed the lion over and continued its angry march toward us. It would be on top of us in seconds.

I watched my chest heave up and down and tried to catch my breath. I only had one more chance before it was game over. I closed my eyes and pushed my hands back and up again. It had to work this time. It had to. I drove my hands toward the back of my chair as hard as I could again but this time knowing it was the last chance I had.

My hands were free! The zip tie fell apart and dropped to the floor.

But it was too late.

The bear was almost on top of Darryl. There was nothing I could do to save him. My only option was to try to get my mom out while the bear overtook him. No, that wasn't my only option.

What was it Amanda had said? Oh, yeah. I was a time sorter. I could slow time down or speed it up like a flip book. I just had to learn how to control it.

I closed my eyes and took a deep breath. Slow … slow … slow…

I reopened my eyes and watched the room around me fall into slow motion. Saliva danced in the air from the bear's mouth as it growled.

I had time to think. It would be at least ten seconds before the bear devoured Darryl while time was slowed.

I could break his zip tie. Then I'd have to help him up and move him out of the way. And we'd still have to run for our lives.

No. That wouldn't work.

I could break open the rifle cabinet, load the gun, and shoot the bear. It was all the way across the room.

No. That wouldn't work.

I concentrated on making time go even slower. It didn't work.

Five seconds left. It was almost the end of the flip book.

The bear had already disregarded my mom. Bad Dude didn't have any more use for her. He only wanted me, Darryl, and Amanda. Right now, the only person I could save was Darryl.

Two seconds left before time returned to normal.

My heart raced. There was only one way to protect him, and it required a sacrifice that scared me more than anything. I lifted my feet and did the only thing there was enough time left to do.

I dived between the bear and Darryl just before the beast tore into him with its teeth, covering

Darryl's body with mine. I wasn't more important than anyone else. This was the end.

*Bang *Bang *Bang *Bang *Bang *Bang

The bear howled in pain as the sound of gunshots filled the room. It turned away from us and barreled toward the sliding glass door then straight through it, glass shattering inside and out.

I stood back up and looked across the room to see my mom standing with a handgun still pointed in the bear's direction. It was the same gun she always kept by her ankle.

"Nobody messes with my kid," she said before she dropped the gun. And then she cried as she reached out her arms for me. I had never been so impressed by my mom. I made sure Darryl was okay then rushed to her side and hugged her as hard as I could, thankful that I hadn't lost her.

"We need to talk," she said as she sat on the floor, looking exhausted. I was willing to listen because I knew it was really her this time. I sat right next to her as she folded her arms over her knees. "Before you were born, I fell in love with the kindest, gentlest, strongest man I had ever known." She smiled at distant memories. "He had a baby girl that

I loved and thought of as my own daughter. I married that man, completely in love with him, thinking that we'd be together forever.

"After a while, he started talking about another planet and how he was the king. He said his people were in danger, and he was trying to find another planet for them." She focused her eyes on the stuffed elephant in front of us. "I didn't believe him. I thought he was trying to get out of our marriage."

I tried to register what she was saying. She knew about planet Amagrandus and all of this craziness for years and never told me?

"He left one day with his daughter, who had the most beautiful green eyes. She was so innocent and only a baby. He said it was too dangerous for me if he stayed, and it wasn't my burden to bear. I begged him not to go." She wiped a tear from her eye. "I never saw him or his daughter again."

"Why are you telling me this now?" I asked her, angry and confused. She had known about Amanda's planet my entire life and had never said anything about it.

"That man is your father, Jake," she said bluntly. "I found out I was pregnant with you a week after he left."

The room seemed to spin around my head, making me dizzy. "If he's my father ... then Amanda is my sister." Now it made sense why I had a connection with her and why I had wanted to protect her so badly.

My mom leaned toward me and wrapped an arm around my shoulders. "I tried to find them for so many years, but they vanished ... like they left this planet."

"Does John know about this?" I asked. I hoped my stepdad didn't know more than me about my own past.

She shook her head. "I know you've always felt different, like you don't fit in. It's torn at me for so long not to tell you what the truth might be. Even if I wasn't sure ... until now."

Darryl's chair squeaked from across the room. "He's going to hurt the princess." My mom and I got up to check on him now that he was lucid again. "Tony ... he's going to take Princess Amanda back to Amagrandus and force her to face trial before Prince Badood. She'll be executed."

Before I could say anything, my mom stepped in

front of me and asked him, "Why did your people come back after all these years? You've put my son in danger."

Darryl huffed and shook his head. "Prince Badood discovered that the king has a son on this planet. He's here to destroy your son." He looked around my mother and straight at me. "Princess Amanda demanded that we come here to protect you when she discovered the truth."

My mom bent down and studied Darryl's arms and legs. They were covered in scrapes and bruises. "There may be some medical supplies in the bathroom or somewhere around here. I'll check." She patted me on the shoulder before she walked out of the room.

"You have royal blood," Darryl said, coughing up dirt. "You are the rightful heir to the throne, the only one who can help me save the princess and the king." He shook his head as if he was ashamed and said, "I'm sorry."

"For what?" He had nothing to be sorry about. I felt scared and empowered, finally knowing what my purpose was. If he hadn't been there, I would have believed everything Prince Bad Dude had said through my mom's mouth.

"For the lunch tray and getting you into trouble at school," he said. "I was angry because I didn't want you to know the truth. You already had a perfect life and this one is too dangerous. I didn't think you could handle it." He looked into my eyes and nodded. "I was wrong."

My mom came back into the room with bandages and medical supplies. She cut the zip tie binding Darryl's hands.

"Prince Jake," he said, falling to one knee from his chair, bowing to me.

"Stand up," I demanded. No one needed to bow before me. I wasn't better than anyone else. I was still the same person, and he was Amanda's cousin, making him my cousin too. "We are equals. It's time to end this."

My mom's face was flushed, like she was scared for me. I knew she still saw me as a little kid, but now I was ready to do whatever I had to do so I could protect everyone.

"It's okay," I assured her. "I know who I am now." She nodded hesitantly.

Darryl put a hand on my shoulder. "Let's save the

princess."

I put a hand on his and glanced at my mom. "Let's save my sister."

ELEVEN

A SPACESHIP
AND A WAY OUT

It wasn't dark outside yet, but the sun was halfway down the sky. My mom drove her car back into our hometown while Darryl guided her to where he, Amanda, and Tony had first come to the city.

"I hope we're not too late," Darryl whispered. He led us to a side of town that was used for farming. I had been out here once before, but there was no reason to come back because it was mostly grass and trees for miles. We passed by cows, chickens, and goats in the fields. We even passed by a peanut processing factory.

"Here," Darryl said, pointing to an almost invisible driveway on the side of the road, overgrown with weeds and flowers. "Turn here."

My mom drove slowly through the grassy driveway, unable to see far in front of us with thick weeds that were taller than the windshield. She drove for what seemed like miles in the dense vegetation that never seemed to end. "Are you sure?" she asked Darryl. He nodded.

When the overgrown weeds finally ended, the car stopped in a large field of wildflowers that were yellow, green, blue, orange, purple, red and white. It felt strangely familiar, like I had been here many times before. An old, wooden, two-story red barn sat up ahead on the right. But none of that mattered because straight ahead was something amazing I had never seen before.

"This is it," Darryl said, opening his door and walking into the field.

"You should stay here," I told my mom from the back. She had already been through more than any mom should have to go through and there was no reason for her to get into more danger. She appeared weak after Bad Dude had controlled her mind and body.

She looked back at me and winked. "Not a chance." She opened her door and got out.

"Wait for me!" I shouted after I exited the car. She was almost caught up with Darryl. I was surprised she could even stand. I ran to them and held my breath as we got closer to the massive object in front of us. It was an oval, metallic spaceship as big as the barn. I felt overwhelmed and astounded. I had seen similar UFOs in movies, but they usually came with little green aliens inside of them.

A loud tractor rumbled from in front of the farmhouse. It vibrated as if it was gassed up and ready to go, but no one was anywhere near it. It was hard to hear anything over the roar of the motor without shouting.

"It's still here," Darryl said, seeming relieved. "There's still time." He held a hand up to me and my mom, telling us to stay where we were as he approached the ship. He spread out his fingers and placed his hand on the metallic skin. A door retracted from the bottom of it and let him in. He stepped inside and disappeared.

We waited for him for what felt like minutes. My mom leaned against the ship to keep her balance as the door that had opened for Darryl closed. We couldn't see or hear anything that was going on inside. Had he found Amanda? Was Tony in there? I spread out my fingers and placed my hand on the ship the same way that Darryl had. Nothing happened.

The door finally opened again, and he stepped out, shaking his head. "They're not inside."

"We need to search the barn," I insisted.

"Someone turned that tractor on today." I doubted they were inside, but I didn't care if we had to sleep in the barn, I was not going to let Tony take my sister away in that ship. We would wait and we'd be ready for him.

Darryl and my mom agreed. "First," he said, "let's turn the tractor off. It's giving me a headache." He placed his hand on the ship again to close the door before heading toward the tractor. My mom kept a hand on my shoulder as we trudged along with him through the wildflowers. As soon as we reached the tractor, he turned the key and restored peaceful silence.

"Help!" a hoarse-sounding female shouted from inside the barn.

"Amanda!" I shouted back, racing for the barn doors. She was inside!

Darryl stopped me before I unhooked the latch holding the doors closed. "We don't know if Prince Badood is in control. Let's do this together." I agreed with him. My mom stayed behind and sat against the barn, waving to let me know that she'd be okay as we pulled the doors open.

Amanda sat in a chair in the middle of the empty barn. Her hands were bound behind her back with old rope. Her face was red from the heat.

Darryl tried to hold me back, but I raced to her. Tony was probably around, but I couldn't let my sister suffer for another second. I untied the rope as quickly as I could and helped her to her feet.

"Jake," she said to me, seeming surprised, "you came for me."

"I promised to protect you," I reminded her.

She sighed and said, "There's something I have to tell you."

I smiled at her, knowing what it was. "You're my sister."

She smiled back and her eyes sparkled green. "And you're my brother."

Suddenly, a loud engine roared from outside the barn. It was much more powerful than the tractor.

"The ship!" Darryl yelled as he raced back outside.

My heart stopped as I looked outside the barn. "Where's my mom?" Amanda grabbed my hand

and ran with me to join Darryl.

Out in the field, in front of the ship, Tony stood before the open door of the metallic UFO, holding my mom firmly by his side. Her hands were bound behind her back. She looked weak and helpless next to him. They were almost inside, too late for us to reach them.

"Stop!" I yelled out to him. This couldn't be happening. He was so deranged that he wanted me to see my mom struggle. It was hard to see her that way because she had prepared my entire life for a moment like this, but Bad Dude had taken all her strength.

He turned and winked at me. "You're not as smart as you thought," he taunted me. "Your mom will face trial and be executed because of you and your family."

Amanda threw out her hands to fire a green bolt of lightning at him, but he grabbed my mom and shoved her in front of him as a shield. Amanda balled her fists and screamed. "Why are you doing this? I command you to let her go!"

He walked backward, pulling my mom with him and putting one foot into the ship. "You command me? My family has been loyal to yours for generations." He fell silent for a few seconds.

I closed my eyes and concentrated on everything moving slower. I needed more time to save my mom. I was angry and sad and scared. I had never felt so overwhelmed with so many emotions at one time. I couldn't focus.

I reopened my eyes. Everything around me was still moving at a normal speed. "It's not working!" I shouted to Amanda.

"Jake, honey," my mom called out, tears streaming down her face. "I love you more than anything." Tony snatched her to the side and shoved her into the ship.

"Prince Badood has made me royalty," he claimed, smiling at me and Amanda. "You will now suffer at my feet." Amanda threw green lightning at him, but he ducked inside and closed the door before it reached him. The green lightning deflected off the door.

Darryl rushed to the ship and placed his hand on it to get inside, but he was locked out. He held his hands out to control the ship and keep it from flying away, but it was way more powerful than my lunch tray or the jaguar had been. He banged his fists on it and screamed in frustration. Fire erupted from beneath the ship and threw him back as it lifted into the air.

"No!" I shouted, running toward the ship. "No!" The ship shot up into the clouds then zoomed off at an angle and disappeared.

I fell to my knees and stared up at the empty sky.

"Mom? Mom!" I screamed louder and stronger than I ever had before. "No!" My pulse raced so fast that I couldn't breathe. My fingers turned red after I balled them into fists tighter than they were meant to be. "Mom … Mom … Mom…"

Light flashed in front of me and a door I had seen thousands of times appeared in the field of wildflowers. Orange light flooded through cracks in the wooden frame. It was the door from my dreams. It was real.

I wiped the tears from my eyes and stood up slowly. "My father's door," I whispered, walking toward it. Amanda appeared by my side and grabbed my hand again, nodding confidently. Darryl appeared on my other side.

"I failed you," he said with his head down. "I'm

sorry, Prince Jake." I patted his shoulder and shook my head, knowing it wasn't his fault but unable to form words yet. My throat felt raw.

As we approached the door, Amanda and Darryl stopped. They tried to move forward, but something held them back. I looked at Amanda, not wanting to do this alone.

"We can't go with you," she said apologetically. "It's only meant for one person. Father used this to travel through space and time, and I went with him as a baby and toddler in search of a safer world. Only you can enter it now." I had never been able to enter it in my dreams so I wasn't convinced I could enter it in real life.

"What do I do if I get inside?" I asked, having no idea what waited behind the door.

"Concentrate on a time and place you want to be in as you walk through the door," Amanda advised. "You will go there immediately."

I placed my hand on the doorknob and turned it. It turned for the first time! My mind filled with possibilities of when and where I could go.

"Jake," Amanda called out softly before I opened the door, "you never had to go through any of this.

You should go back to a time before you ever sat at our lunch table."

I thought about that. I could go all the way back to kindergarten, like I had always dreamed. I'd restart my life by becoming the best at sports and making friends. I'd study harder and get more A's and B's than C's. I'd finally be popular. I wouldn't have to face the jaguar, the monkey, the dinosaur, the bear, and especially not Prince Bad Dude masquerading as my mom. "What about you? What's going to happen to you?"

She glanced at Darryl and nodded. "Once you step through that door, you'll be the only one who remembers what happened after the time you return to. You won't be in any danger. You won't be chased by wild animals. And you won't have me to bug you as a sister." She chuckled nervously. "We'll still protect you from afar. We'll just never know that we had once met you."

But who's going to protect you? I swallowed hard and pulled the door fully open. Orange light flooded out and consumed my body. I took a deep breath and concentrated on the most important moment of my life as I stepped into the unknown.

"Goodbye, brother," I heard Amanda whisper, weeping, as the door closed behind me and my world went dark.

*****

I blinked one time and then I was no longer inside the door. The big red barn stood behind me. Amanda was on one side of me and Darryl on the other. The spaceship was in front of us as it had been before. My mother was within running distance, held captive by Tony.

"Your mom will face trial and be executed because of you and your family," he called out.

Amanda threw out her hands to fire a green bolt of lightning at him, but he grabbed my mom and shoved her in front of him as a shield, just like before. Amanda balled her fists and screamed. "Why are you doing this? I command you to let her go!"

He walked backward, pulling my mom with him and putting one foot into the ship. "You command me? My family has been loyal to yours for generations."

This was the moment I came back for. It had to work. "Mom!" I shouted. "Bridge!" I had thought about the night before when she pretended to put a bridge over my head at the dinner table. She looked confused at first but then bent down and ducked.

"Amanda," I said to her quickly. "Now!"

She didn't waste a second and threw out her hands to fire green lightning at Tony. It slammed into his chest and knocked him over, almost into the ship.

Darryl rushed up to him and pulled him back. "Oh, no you don't."

I ran to my mom and wrapped my arms around her. I never wanted to let her go again. Amanda joined us and helped me untie her. The three of us hugged.

"We did it," I said, hardly believing it myself.

"Together, we are unstoppable," Amanda added.

Darryl held Tony in a vice grip and said, "We'll stop Prince Bad Dude"—he winked at me—"and restore the kingdom."

We all looked up when forked lightning flashed throughout the sky, setting it on fire as night approached. Thunder boomed and the ground rumbled.

Tony began to laugh and didn't stop as the

thunder got louder. "You're too late. Badood has arrived."

Amanda grabbed my hand as the sky turned the darkest I had ever seen it. "Are you ready for this?" she asked.

I stared up at the darkened sky with her, wondering what was going to happen next. After a day like today, I was ready for anything.

AMAGRANDUS FOREVER

The lightning and thunder had stopped, and the earth remained still and silent the rest of the night. I studied the intricate details and superior craftsmanship of the ginormous spaceship, a reminder of where I was and where I could be. Was I supposed to go back with Amanda, Darryl, and Tony to claim my rightful place as Prince of Amagrandus or was I supposed to stay here? And were they planning to go back or stay put for a while?

"We'll figure it out," my mom said, sensing the worry on my face. She seemed stronger. "Let's savor the victory for now." She always had the right answers.

"If Prince Badood is coming here or is here already, he's not just here for us," Amanda said, nodding at Darryl. "He's here to destroy this planet."

"It's true," Darryl confirmed. "Badood will conquer any planet he can and steal its resources." He turned to me. "He and your father were once friends. When the king refused to destroy other planets, Badood turned against him."

"That's why he went back," my mom whispered, realizing the truth. "Blayne wanted to protect this planet and all the others."

"And he was imprisoned for it," Darryl said. "Badood won't be alone when he comes," he warned. "He must have restored the master ship. He'll bring thousands of soldiers with him."

I gulped. "Soldiers? Thousands?" The feeling of victory had been short-lived. There were only five of us, including my mom, and Tony didn't count.

"Not so cocky now, are you?" Tony mocked. "We did it," he said in a high-pitched whiny voice, pretending to be me. Darryl glared at him and tightened the rope around his wrists.

"This isn't our fight," Darryl said to Amanda. "We should head home while Badood is distracted. It will give us the advantage we need to reclaim the throne."

She glanced at me, seeing the disappointment in my eyes. Maybe my rightful place was on another planet, but I wouldn't let my friends and family on Earth suffer because of me. I couldn't leave and I wouldn't, regardless of what she chose to do. "I'm not running from this," Amanda declared. "I'll stay and fight."

I nodded at her, respecting her decision and admiring her bravery.

"Then we fight," Darryl proclaimed. "Amagrandus forever!"

"Amagrandus forever!" Amanda and I shouted after him.

Lights flashed in the dark through the thick wildflowers before the open field.

"Who else knows we're here?" Darryl asked Tony, holding him by the shirt collar. Tony laughed at him and shrugged.

My heart stopped. Had Bad Dude and his soldiers found us already? I wasn't prepared to face him yet. Sure, I was a time sorter, but there were so many things I didn't know or understand about it yet. Maybe we needed to hop on the ship and fly out of there. I was not going to let anyone take my mom away from me again.

Amanda and Darryl stood by my side, staring into the wildflowers, waiting to see who or what came out. My mom rolled up her sleeves and stood strong. My knees were wobbly, but this was my family, and I'd forever stand with them.

Two headlights broke through the darkness. They appeared to belong to a large vehicle like a truck or SUV. The headlights inched slowly toward us.

The vehicle stopped twenty-five feet in front of us, and a man jumped out of the front seat. He left the driver's door open as he walked through the streaming headlights and toward us. I could only see the outline of his body, which got clearer as he got closer. Something about him was familiar.

"Hello, kids," he said in a voice I definitely knew from somewhere. When he was at arm's length, there was no mistaking the smile he had that never went away. Even at night, in the middle of nowhere, he wore a gray suit with a gray tie. It was Mr. Spradley, the vice principal that had sent me to the front of the school cafeteria. "Your father sent me to help," he said, looking from Amanda to me.

"Amagrandus forever."

THE END
AND THE BEGINNING

No Alien Was Harmed In The Making
Of This Book.

Not That I Know Of.

MY EPIC ADVICE TO YOU

#1

Don't play dodgeball with jaguars. They're nothing but cheetahs.

MY EPIC ADVICE TO YOU

#2

If a vulture stares at you, pretend you're invisible. Seriously, cover your face.

MY EPIC ADVICE TO YOU

#3

If a dinosaur has bad breath, give it a mint. Or run. Yeah, you should run.

MY EPIC ADVICE TO YOU

#4

If you're in a room full of bears, lions, rhinoceros, and buffalo - play possum.

>>>>

MY EPIC ADVICE TO YOU

#5

Always carry a hot dog with you so baby alligators don't mistake your fingers for hot dogs.

MY EPIC ADVICE TO YOU

#6

Don't play with monkeys in parking lots. They'll go bananas and eat your apple.

MY EPIC ADVICE TO YOU

#7

Don't get into spaceships with aliens you don't know. Even if they offer you space candy.

>>>>

MY EPIC ADVICE TO YOU

#8

If your lunch tray flies off the table, remain calm. The food wasn't good anyway.

 >>>>

MY EPIC ADVICE TO YOU

#9

If your dog scratches at the window and whines when you leave, stay home!

A note to all kids and parents

Thank you so much for taking the time to read this story! You're Awesome! You're Epic! I hope you enjoyed reading this as much as I enjoyed writing it, and I'd be eternally grateful if you'd leave a review on Amazon and Goodreads to let me know what you think about **Epic Kids**. Your review helps other readers like yourself find this book and enjoy it.

Be sure to click the Follow button next to my name (David Blaze) on Amazon to be notified when my sequels and new books are released.

You can find me on Facebook as:
David Blaze, Children's Author

You can find my books and contact me at:
www.davidblazebooks.com

Check out these other award-winning books for young readers by David Blaze!

About the Author

Timothy David and his son Zander Blaze live in Orlando, Florida with their crazy dog (Sapphire) and Zander's awesome mom! Timothy David loves to watch funny movies and eat pizza rolls! Zander Blaze loves to play with Hot Wheels and feast on chicken nuggets! Together, as David Blaze, they share lots of laughs and have lots of fun.

Wow! That's EPIC!

David Blaze

Made in the USA
San Bernardino, CA
21 May 2020